I'm the Best Artist in the OCEAN

by Kevin Sherry

Dial Books for Young Readers

Hello!
I'm a GIANT squid!

I can

DRAW!!

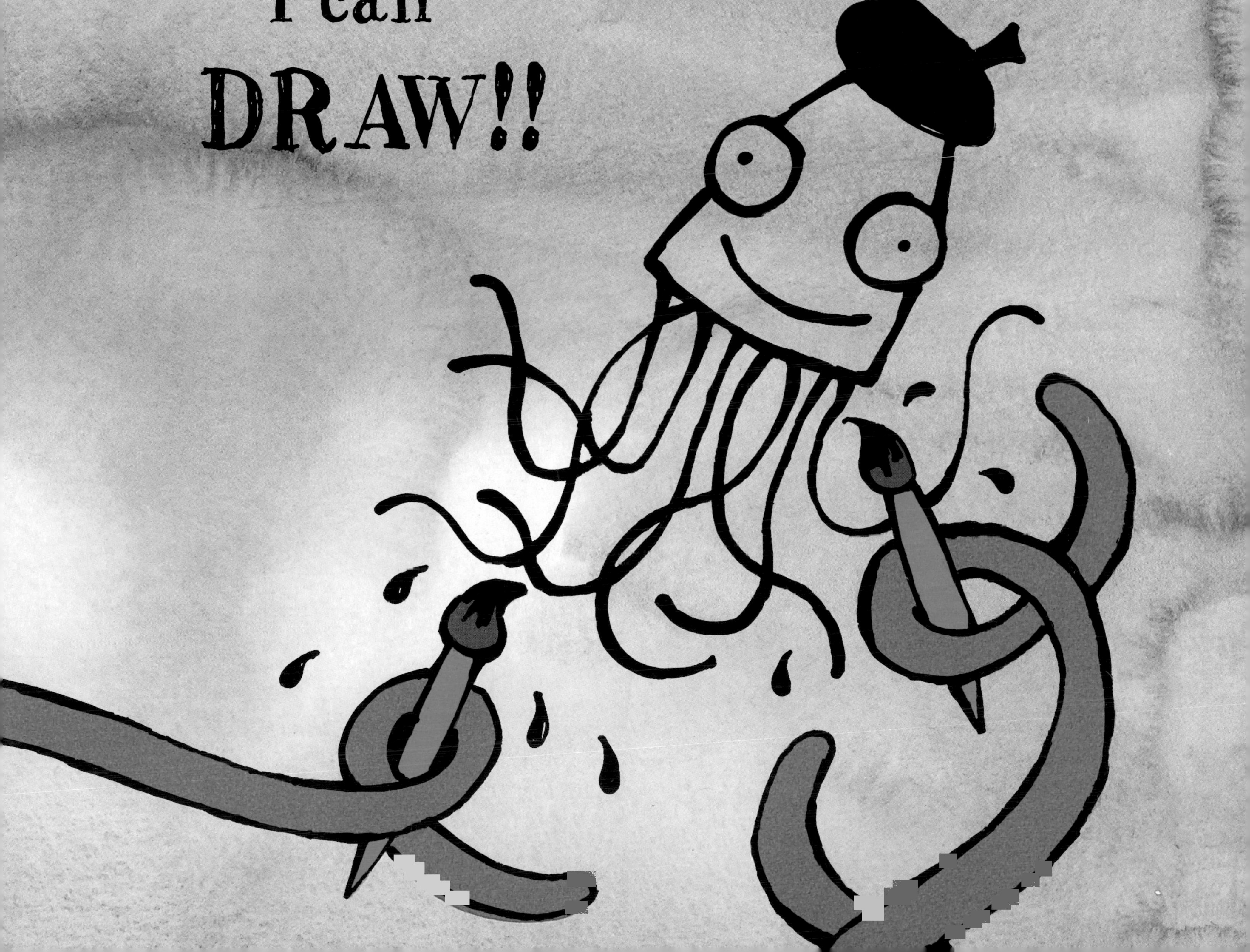

I can draw fish,

I can
draw
crabs,

and
jellyfish!

I'm making my
MASTERPIECE!!

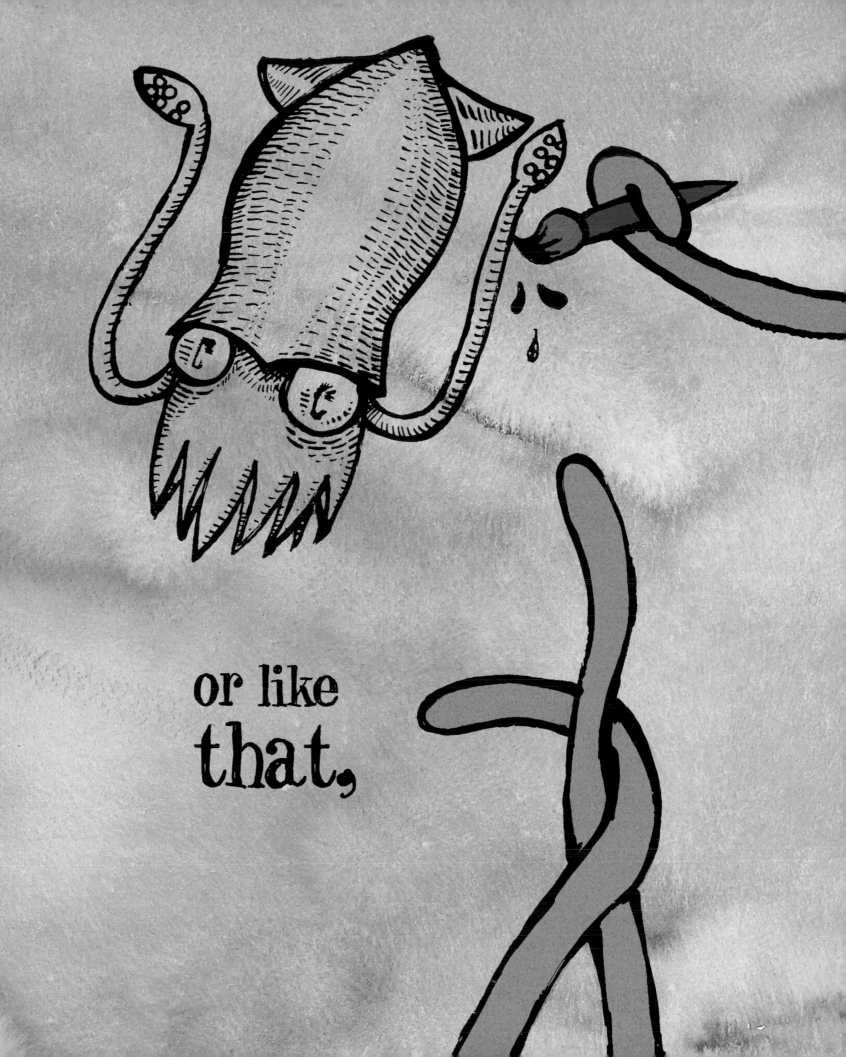

or even
like
that!

I'm the **BEST ARTIST** in the **OCEAN!!**

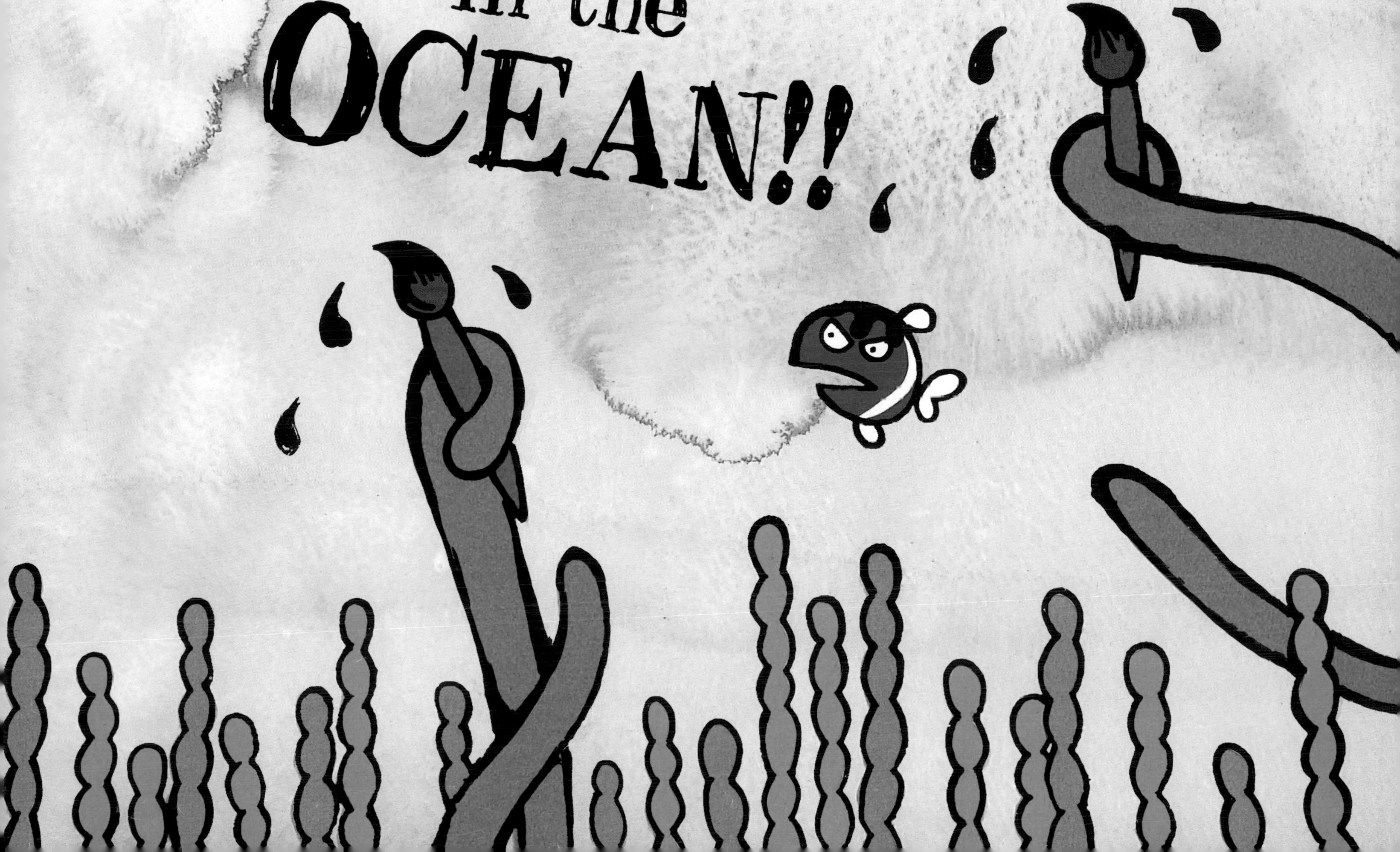

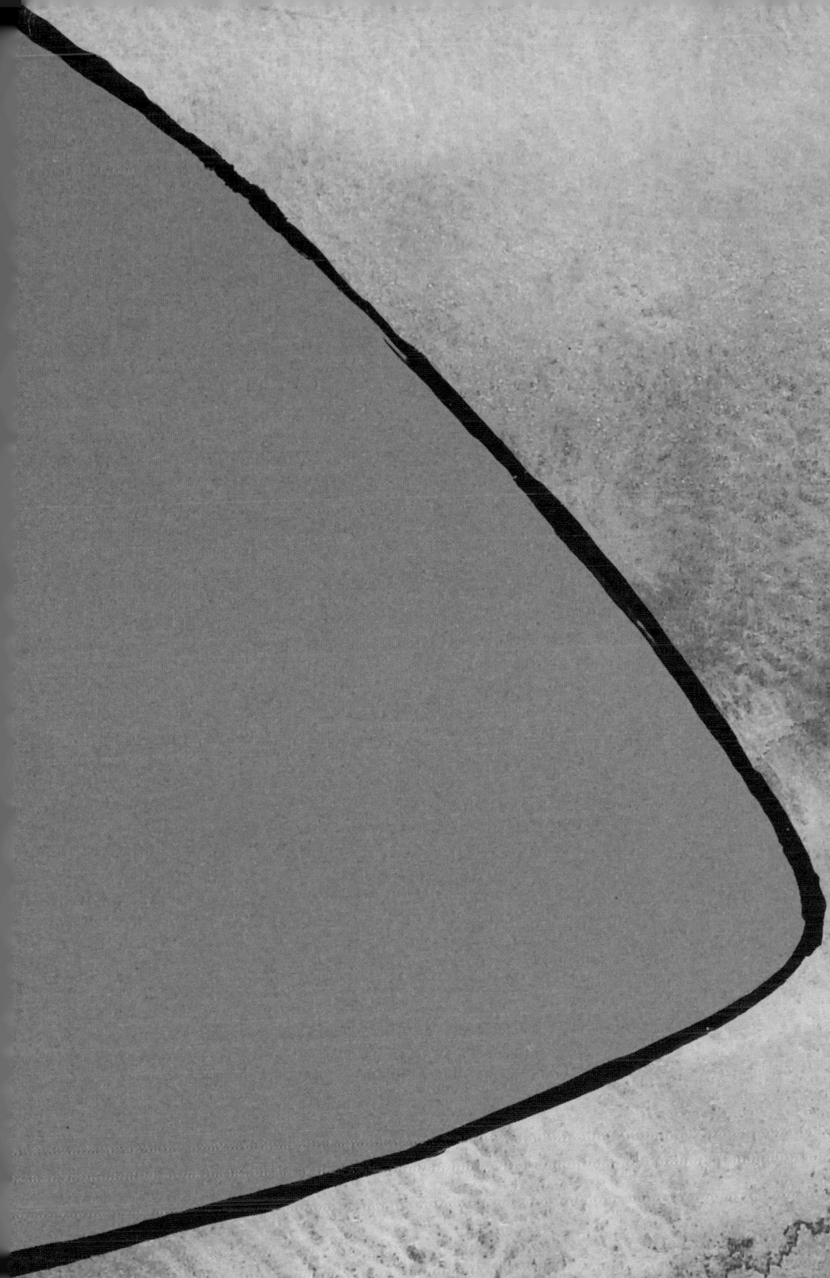

STOP!

You mean . . .

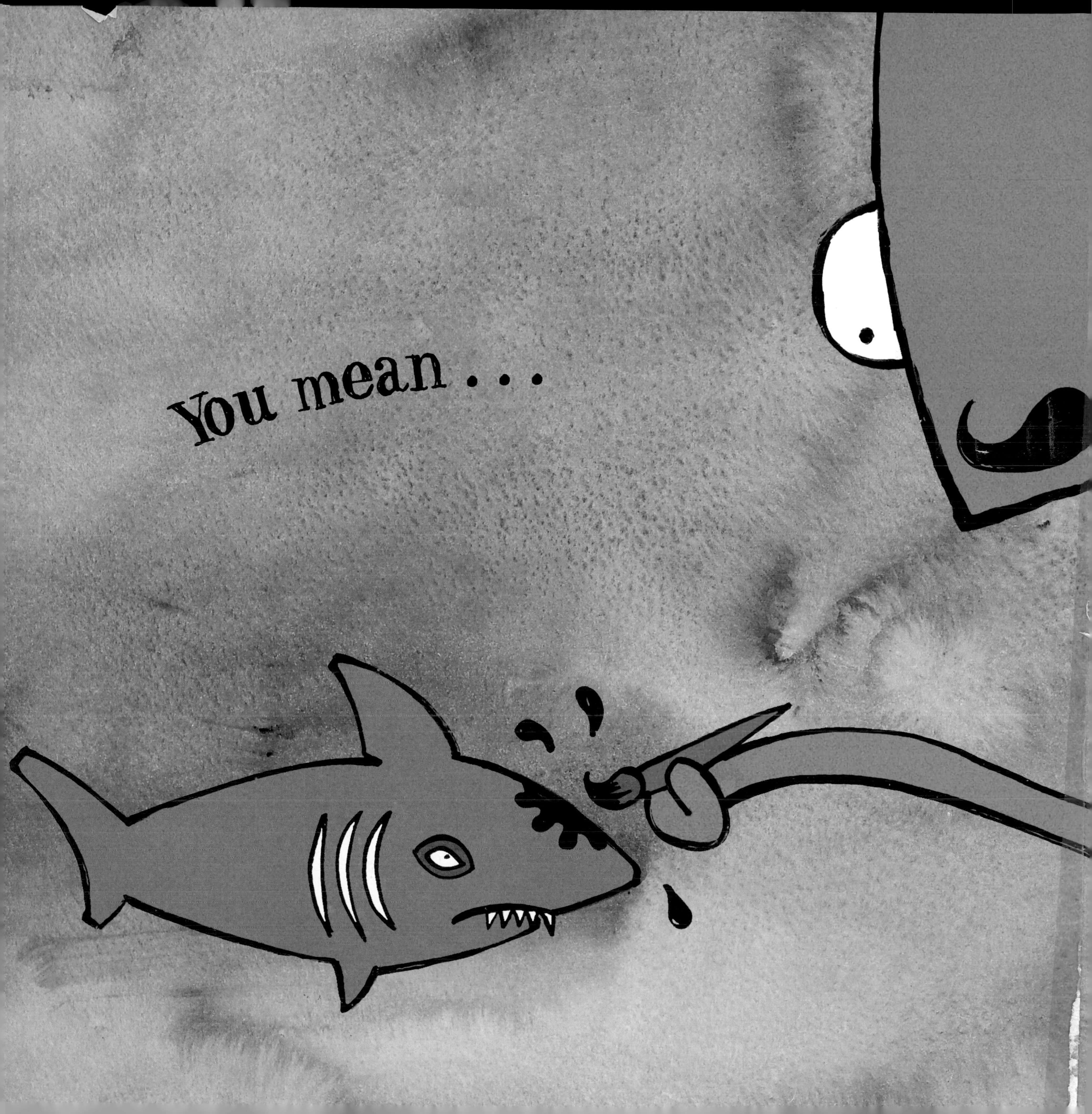

**To Bettiann Young, Ron George, Akiko Day,
and all the other incredible teachers
who have inspired me on my artistic voyage**

DIAL BOOKS FOR YOUNG READERS • A division of Penguin Young Readers Group • Published by The
Penguin Group • Penguin Group (USA) Inc., 375 Hudson Street, New York, NY 10014, U.S.A. • Penguin Group
(Canada), 90 Eglinton Avenue East, Suite 700, Toronto, Ontario, Canada M4P 2Y3 (a division of Pearson
Penguin Canada Inc.) • Penguin Books Ltd, 80 Strand, London WC2R 0RL, England • Penguin Ireland,
25 St. Stephen's Green, Dublin 2, Ireland (a division of Penguin Books Ltd) • Penguin Group (Australia),
250 Camberwell Road, Camberwell, Victoria 3124, Australia (a division of Pearson Australia Group Pty Ltd)
• Penguin Books India Pvt Ltd, 11 Community Centre, Panchsheel Park, New Delhi - 110 017, India • Penguin
Group (NZ), 67 Apollo Drive, Rosedale, North Shore 0632, New Zealand (a division of Pearson New Zealand Ltd)
• Penguin Books (South Africa) (Pty) Ltd, 24 Sturdee Avenue, Rosebank, Johannesburg 2196, South Africa
Penguin Books Ltd, Registered Offices: 80 Strand, London WC2R 0RL, England

Designed by Teresa Kietlinski Dikun & Kimi Weart

Text set in Bookman, Blue Century

Manufactured in China on acid-free paper

10 9 8 7 6 5

Library of Congress Cataloging-in-Publication Data available upon request

The art was completed in three layers, each separated by glass that was pried from the windows
of shipwrecked pirate ships. There is a watercolor layer background, then a cut-paper level, and finally,
an ink layer consisting of 100% fresh squid ink. The endpapers are modeled after Joan Miró's *Poetess*
and the whale mural after Pablo Picasso's *Guernica*.